WITHDRAWN

P9-EGN-713

Magic Puppy

To Champion—wonderful and steadfast

GROSSET & DUNLAP
Published by the Penguin Group
Penguin Group (USA) LLC, 375 Hudson Street, New York, New York 10014, USA

USA | Canada | UK | Ireland | Australia | New Zealand | India | South Africa | China

penguin.com
A Penguin Random House Company

If you purchased this book without a cover, you should be aware that this book is stolen property. It was reported as "unsold and destroyed" to the publisher, and neither the author nor the publisher has received any payment for this "stripped book."

Penguin supports copyright. Copyright fuels creativity, encourages diverse voices, promotes free speech, and creates a vibrant culture. Thank you for buying an authorized edition of this book and for complying with copyright laws by not reproducing, scanning, or distributing any part of it in any form without permission. You are supporting writers and allowing Penguin to continue to publish books for every reader.

Text copyright © 2009 Sue Bentley. Illustrations copyright © 2009 Angela Swan. Cover illustration © 2009 Andrew Farley. First printed in Great Britain in 2009 by Penguin Books Ltd. First published in the United States in 2014 by Grosset & Dunlap, a division of Penguin Young Readers Group, 345 Hudson Street, New York, New York 10014. GROSSET & DUNLAP is a trademark of Penguin Group (USA) LLC. Printed in the U.S.A.

Library of Congress Cataloging-in-Publication Data is available.

ISBN 978-0-448-46791-7   10 9 8 7 6 5 4 3 2 1

Sunshine Shimmers

SUE BENTLEY

Illustrated by Angela Swan

Grosset & Dunlap
An Imprint of Penguin Group (USA) LLC

Prologue

The young silver-gray wolf raised his head and looked up at the mountaintops, which were veiled by mist. Storm took a deep breath. It felt good to be back. He wondered where his mother might be hiding.

Suddenly a terrifying howl shattered the silence.

"Shadow!" Storm gasped, realizing that

the fierce lone wolf who had attacked his family and the Moon-claw pack was very close.

There was a bright flash and a dazzling shower of golden sparks. Where Storm had been standing, there now crouched a tiny fluffy ginger-and-black Yorkshire terrier puppy with a pointed face, pricked ears, and midnight blue eyes.

Storm trembled, hoping that his puppy disguise would protect him from the evil Shadow. Keeping his furry belly close to the ground, Storm crept toward a clump of rocks.

As he approached, one of the rocks seemed to move. Storm's tiny heart beat fast as he picked out the shape of a large adult wolf and saw the gleam of familiar bright golden eyes.

The tiny puppy's whole body wriggled and his tail twirled. "Mother!" Storm yapped with relief. With a whimper of greeting, he leaped forward and began licking Canista's mouth and nose.

"I am glad you are safe and well, my son, but you have returned at a dangerous time," Canista said in a warm, velvety growl. She nuzzled her disguised cub's little ginger-and-black face, but then gave a sharp wince of pain.

"Let me help you!" Storm blew out a gentle stream of tiny gold sparks, which swirled around a nasty bite on Canista's leg for a few seconds and then disappeared.

"Thank you, Storm. The pain is easing. But there isn't time now for you to help me recover all my powers as well. You must go—Shadow is very close," Canista rumbled softly.

Sadness rippled through Storm's tiny puppy body as he thought of his father and brothers and the once proud Moon-claw wolves, now gone or scattered. His midnight blue eyes flashed with anger. "One day I will stand beside you and face Shadow and force him to leave our lands forever!"

Canista nodded proudly. "And then the others will accept you as their leader, and the Moon-claw pack will run together again. But until then you must use this disguise and hide in the other world. Return when you are wiser and your magic is stronger."

Another fierce howl split the air. The sound of iron-hard paws thundered on the hillside. Powerful claws scrabbled at the rocks, close to where Storm and his mother hid. "I know you are here! Let us finish this!" Shadow growled coldly.

"Go now, Storm! Save yourself!" Canista urged.

Bright gold sparks ignited in the tiny puppy's ginger-and-black fur. Storm whined softly as he felt the power gathering inside him. Golden light pooled brightly around him. It grew brighter . . .

Chapter
ONE

Della Walton sighed as she sat next to her mom in the busy Valencia airport.

"Cheer up, honey," her mom said. "I'm sure our luggage will turn up. Your dad's gone to find someone who can help to track it down."

"I know. But it's not just that," Della said dejectedly, thinking about Chloe, who was originally supposed to come with

them on their trip to Spain. But at the last
minute, Della's younger cousin had decided
that she'd miss her parents too much and
was staying at home. Della was certain
that the vacation wasn't going to be half as
much fun without Chloe to play with.

"I know you're disappointed about
your cousin, but I'm sure you'll meet some
new friends," her mom said.

Della hoped so. She tried to smile, for her mom's sake, but she couldn't make herself cheer up. It felt like a big black cloud was hanging over her head.

She saw her dad weaving toward them through the crowds of people. "Well, that was a waste of time," he said, irritated. "A whole lot of luggage has gone missing, and no one has any idea where it is. We're supposed to go on to the villa, and the airport staff will get in touch when our things turn up. I've left them our contact information."

"Oh, dear. Well, I suppose we'd better pick up the car and get going," Mrs. Walton said in her calm, practical way. "It's a good thing we've got our money and all the important stuff."

Della trudged after her mom and

dad as they stepped outside the airport terminal. Bright sunshine shone down on beds of palm trees and giant cacti.

They picked up their car and soon joined the busy traffic on the highway.

Della stared gloomily out of the window at the towns they passed, baking in the sun, and the lines of cars and huge

trucks. After about twenty minutes, the traffic thinned out, and the scenery was replaced by shady groves of olive and orange trees and green fields with low farmhouses.

Overhead, the sky was a clear, bright blue. Despite herself, Della gradually felt her spirits starting to lift a bit. She was about to ask if they were there yet when they turned on to a narrow road that snaked up the side of a hill.

"There's our villa!" Mrs. Walton said, pointing.

Della caught a glimpse of white walls and a red-tiled roof through the trees. Maybe things would get better once they got there. She began looking forward to a long, cool drink as she relaxed and splashed around in the pool.

But as their car drew to a halt outside the villa, Della caught her breath. Metal shutters covered all the windows, the lawn was long and straggly, and the pool was a sludgy greenish color.

"You must have made a mistake, Dad! This is the wrong place!" she exclaimed. There was no way she was swimming in *that* pool!

Scratching his head, her dad checked the address. "No. This is it, all right. I don't understand what's gone wrong. The owner lives on a farm just down the road." He turned to his wife. "Why don't you and Della relax in the shade while I go and have a word with her?"

Mrs. Walton nodded. "Good idea." She got out of the car and then sank onto a wooden bench beneath a tree.

I'm going to have a look around, Della decided, wandering off down a winding path past some flower beds. "First I'm left with no one to play with and now the villa's a dump. This vacation's one giant disaster," she grumbled, starting to wish that she'd stayed at home, too. At least then she and Chloe could have had fun together.

She had just reached some palm trees when a dazzling flash lit up the white garden wall.

"Oh!" Della blinked, blinded for a moment. She looked up, expecting to see dark clouds gathering after what she thought was a flash of lightning. But the sky was still calm and sunny.

Feeling puzzled, Della looked back at the trees and saw a tiny cute puppy with

ginger-and-black fur, a pointed face, and huge midnight blue eyes. Hundreds of tiny sparkles, like miniature fireflies, gleamed in its fluffy coat.

She frowned. What was a puppy doing here with the villa closed up and deserted? Maybe its owners had left it behind when they left. "You poor little thing. Are you all alone?" she murmured.

The puppy stood up and shook itself. "Yes, I am. I have come from far away. Can you help me?" it woofed.

Chapter
TWO

Della stared down at the puppy in surprise. The Spanish heat must have made her feel funny—she'd just imagined that it had spoken to her!

She fanned herself with her hands to cool down a little. The puppy was so cute, but her mom had told her it was best not to touch animals abroad. So she sat down on one of the low walls a little way away.

"I suppose you might belong to someone at the farm. Or maybe you're a stray," she said aloud to herself.

"I do not belong to anyone," the puppy woofed.

Della's eyes widened with shock. She almost toppled back off the wall onto her behind. "Y-you r-really can t-talk!" she stammered, straightening up.

The puppy pricked his tiny ears. "All the wolves in my world can talk. My

name is Storm of the Moon–claw pack. What is yours?" it woofed again.

Della gulped. Talking dogs did not just appear to ordinary girls in real life, except in fairy tales. But this puppy had and it was blinking up at her expectantly with the brightest eyes she had ever seen, waiting for her answer.

"I'm D–Della Walton," she found herself replying.

"I am honored to meet you, Della." The puppy bowed his little head. "Where is this place?" Despite his tiny size, Della noticed that Storm seemed strangely unafraid of her.

"It's a villa in Spain. I'm here on vacation with my parents. At least, we're supposed to be on vacation. So far, everything's gone wrong," she said. She frowned and looked around nervously. "Did . . . did you just say something about a wolf pack?"

Storm nodded proudly. "My mother and father led our Moon-claw pack. But an evil lone wolf attacked us. He is called Shadow. My father and brothers were killed, and my mother is wounded and in hiding. Shadow wants to be leader of our pack, but the others are waiting for me to return. I am here alone in this world."

"But how can you lead a wolf pack? You're a tiny pup—" Della stopped as Storm held up a tiny fluffy front paw and began backing away.

There was another dazzling bright flash, and a burst of gold sparks showered over Della, crackling around her feet onto the grass.

Della rubbed her eyes, and when she could see again, the tiny ginger-and-black puppy was gone. In its place now stood an amazing young wolf with thick silver-gray fur and glowing midnight blue eyes.

"Storm?" Della gasped nervously, eyeing the wolf's large teeth and thick neck-ruff that glimmered with hundreds of gold sparks like tiny yellow diamonds.

"Yes, Della, it is me," Storm said in a deep, velvety growl. "Do not be afraid."

Before Della could get used to seeing Storm as a handsome silver wolf, there was a final gold flash and he again appeared as a cute, fluffy ginger-and-black puppy.

"Wow! You really are a wolf. No one would ever know!" she said, bending

down again and holding out her hand.
Della decided that it would be okay to pet
a magic puppy.

To her delight, Storm edged closer and
brushed her fingers with his damp little
nose. His tail wagged nervously, and she
saw that he was beginning to tremble all
over. "Shadow will know if he finds me.
Will you help me to hide?"

Della's heart went out to the helpless
little puppy. "Of course I will . . ." Her

voice trailed off as she realized that she didn't know what was going to happen with the villa. "Except that I'm not sure where we'll be staying now. I'd love to take you with me, but I don't think Mom will be that happy about me adopting a stray. And I don't see how I can smuggle you into our car without anyone noticing," she said thoughtfully.

"Do not worry. I will use my magic so that only you will be able to see and hear me," Storm woofed.

"You can make yourself invisible? Wow!" Della said breathlessly. "No problem, then. You can stay with me, wherever we end up!"

"Della! Where are you? Your dad's coming back," called her mom's voice.

Della looked around. "Coming!" she

called. She turned back to Storm. "Can you make yourself invisible now?"

Storm nodded. A cloud of tiny gold sparks glittered in his fluffy fur and then went out. "It is done."

As Della began walking back through the garden, Storm padded along invisibly beside her. Della smiled to herself. When her mom had said that she might meet new friends on this vacation, she had never imagined that it would be a magic puppy!

"There's been a mix-up," Della's dad explained. "Maria Isola, who rents out the villa, thought we were arriving next week. She's very sorry and insists that she cooks us all a meal. We can relax at the farm while she and her daughter get the villa ready for us."

Mrs. Walton nodded slowly. "Well, that's good of her. And it will save us trying to find somewhere to eat out."

Storm's probably hungry, too, and ready for a rest after his long journey, Della thought, biting back a grin. She still couldn't quite get used to having the tiny puppy sitting next to her while her mom and dad were completely unaware of him. But as they continued to take no notice of Storm, she felt herself beginning to relax.

Mrs. Walton ruffled Della's short brown hair. "I'm glad you're handling this so well, honey. I know you were already disappointed about Chloe."

"I guess it's not all been that bad," Della said, looking at Storm and smiling to herself.

Her dad grinned. "That's my girl!"

The farmhouse was close by, so they decided to walk to it. "After all, we haven't got any heavy suitcases to carry," Mrs. Walton reasoned.

Della felt better for the first time since their plane had landed. It would have been so cool to share her amazing new secret with Chloe, who she knew would have loved Storm, but Della decided that it was even more special to keep it all to herself. She took her time and let her mom and dad walk ahead of her, enjoying having Storm scampering along beside her on his short ginger-and-black legs.

Della wondered if she still might meet someone her age to be friends with this vacation. *Then,* she thought wistfully, *this could just turn out to be my best vacation ever!*

Chapter
THREE

The farmhouse and buildings were
built around an open-ended courtyard.
Soft early-evening light cast long shadows
across the ground as Della and her family
arrived.

"Oh, it's really pretty," Della said
admiringly, glancing at the stone well and
red and yellow flowers, which glowed
from terra-cotta pots and window boxes.

A dark-haired woman came out of a barn and began scattering handfuls of grain for some chickens that were scratching around in the dust. A smile lit up her face when she spotted Della and her parents.

"That's Mrs. Isola," Della's dad said.

"*Hola!*" the Spanish woman greeted them cheerfully. "Welcome. Come inside. And please call me Maria." After more apologies about the mix-up, Maria made them all cold drinks and then set about making food.

A tall dark-haired girl came into the kitchen. She looked about twelve years old and was carrying a bucket and cleaning things. Maria introduced her as Carmella, her daughter.

"Hi . . . I mean, *hola*," Della said, grinning.

Carmella smiled. "Nice to meet you. I have to start cleaning your villa, but I hope that I will see you later."

"Me too," Della said.

Della quickly made sure that no one was watching her before whispering to Storm, "I'm glad that Carmella and her mom speak English so well. I'm not that great at languages, even though I've been practicing with my Spanish phrase book."

Storm blinked at her with intelligent

bright eyes. "What is a phrase book?"

"It has useful sayings in it, in Spanish, like 'How much is this?' and 'Where can I find a drug store?' But sometimes you can't find the thing you really want to say!"

"I can use my magic to help you to do that," Storm offered helpfully.

"Really? Wow! Thanks. I'll let you know if I need it," Della said. Storm was full of surprises. She wondered what else her amazing little friend could do.

Maria soon rustled up a meal of spicy sausage-and-potato omelets, tomato salad, and crusty bread. Della, Storm, and Della's mom and dad sat at an outside table to eat. After making sure they had everything they needed, Maria went off to join her daughter in getting the villa ready.

The food was delicious. Storm jumped
up to sit on Della's lap, and she was able
to secretly slip bits of food to him. He
gobbled up the omelet and then licked his
chops, seeking out every last tasty morsel
with his little pink tongue.

Della had finished eating and was
stroking Storm's soft fur when suddenly

she felt something hit her lightly on
the side of the head. "Oh!" Puzzled, she
looked around, but couldn't see anything.

Her mom and dad were talking and
hadn't noticed. A moment later something
bounced on to Della's shoulder. This time
an unripe olive landed on the grass next
to her.

Wroo-oof? Storm pricked his ears and
sat up straight, before looking toward
some nearby bushes.

Della followed the tiny puppy's gaze.
She saw the branches move slightly. A girl's
face peeped out, framed by the leaves.
She had blond hair and looked about
eleven years old. Her eyes were sparkling
mischievously.

Della blinked in astonishment. Who
was that? She didn't look like she was part

of Maria's family. Della looked again and
saw the girl put a finger to her pursed lips
before grinning. Della got the message
to stay quiet. She nodded, intrigued. The
branches shifted again and the girl was
hidden from sight.

Storm jumped down and scampered
over to investigate. Della heard him
barking excitedly and then saw him
sniffing around the bushes before running
back toward her.

"The girl has gone," he woofed. "I saw
her run out to the street outside."

Della leaned down and pretended to
fiddle with her flip-flops so that she could
whisper to him. "I wonder who she was.
And how come she's in Maria's garden?"

Storm's midnight blue eyes widened.
"We could follow her and find out. I can
track her scent trail."

Della was tempted—that girl could
be someone her own age to talk to. But
she didn't think her mom and dad would
let her go off by herself when she didn't
know her way around. "I'd better not just
now," she decided.

Mr. Walton stood up and stretched.
"I'm ready to drop. I wonder how soon
we can get into our villa."

"Why don't we walk back and see

how Maria and Carmella are doing?"
Della suggested, thinking that they might
bump into the mystery girl.

"Good idea," her mom said.

The light was already fading as Della
followed them with Storm close at
her heels. Shadows deepened over the
hillside, with its orange and lemon trees
and fields stretching into the distance.
There was no sign of the mystery girl.

At their villa, the windows and doors
were all open. The patio had been swept,
and a table and chairs had been set out.
The smell of freshly cut grass hung in
the air.

Maria met them with a smile.
"Come. I will show you all to your
rooms."

Della, Storm, and Della's parents

followed Maria gratefully up the wooden staircase.

Della's room had white walls and beams across the ceiling. There was a single bed and a matching chest and wardrobe of carved dark wood. Her window had shutters instead of curtains.

Storm began nosing around the room, snuffling up all the interesting smells. He finished exploring and jumped up onto the bed. Sighing contentedly, he curled up

on the cotton blanket and put his nose between his front paws. Della stroked her sleepy friend's soft little head. "You stay there. I'll just pop next door to tell Mom and Dad that I'm having an early night."

As she returned to her bedroom a minute later, a wave of tiredness washed over her. Storm's little snuffly puppy snores were already floating on the air.

He's so sweet, Della whispered to herself as she went to the window. She caught a brief glimpse of another villa through the trees before she closed the shutters and the room was plunged into complete darkness.

Storm's tiny form was gleaming softly on the bed, like a golden nightlight. Della climbed under the cotton sheet and blanket and curled herself around him.

"Night-night. Sleep tight," she whispered.

Grr-rrrf. Storm stirred and opened one sleepy, glowing blue eye and then closed it again.

C h a p t e r
FOUR

"Yay! Our luggage has been found,
and Dad just went to the airport to pick
it up!" Della told Storm excitedly the
following afternoon. "I can get my bathing
suit for a dip in the pool. I was starting
to think that I'd have to spend the whole
vacation in these same jeans and T-shirt."

Storm's little muzzle wrinkled in a
smile and he wagged his tail.

"It feels like the vacation will *really* get much better now," Della commented. "Let's go outside."

Storm followed Della out to where her mom was reading in the garden beyond the pool. Carmella was just leaving after delivering some fresh towels. The older girl smiled at Della and Storm as they walked around the swimming pool.

Della gave her a friendly wave.

Suddenly Storm did a double take and skittered sideways. Della had to swerve to avoid tripping over him. "Oops. Almost fell over my own feet!" she said for Carmella's and her mom's benefit.

Storm stood with his hackles raised, peering down into the murky water. "Come out and fight! Show yourself!" he challenged, growling.

Della felt a faint tingling sensation
flowing down her spine as tiny sparks
began glinting in Storm's fluffy ginger-
and-black fur.

"What is it? What can you see?" she
asked, forgetting to whisper and then she
noticed that the Spanish girl was looking

at her in puzzlement. "I mean . . . I can
see something in the pool! Something's
moving down there!" Della corrected
herself hastily.

Carmella smiled. "That is only the
pool robot. It is an underwater cleaner
that purifies the water. You will be able to
swim in a day or two."

Della hadn't noticed the ridged plastic
tube leading from the generator in the
pool house and disappearing into the
water. "Oh, right," she said, feeling a bit
silly but also disappointed that she still
wouldn't be able to play in the pool. Della
wondered if she and Storm would be
having much fun this week.

Carmella smiled kindly at her and
carried on walking back toward the
farmhouse.

The tingling feeling down Della's back faded as the gold sparks in the tiny puppy's fur went out.

Storm laid back his ears and looked embarrassed. "I am sorry, Della. I did not mean to make a fuss," he yapped apologetically.

Della felt a surge of affection for her brave little friend. "That's okay. You were just trying to protect me, weren't you?"

She wished she could give Storm a cuddle, but she couldn't risk it with her mom so close. "Any good?" Della asked, nodding toward the book her mom was reading.

Her mom smiled. "It's okay. Do you feel like going for a walk? It'll be a while before your dad gets back."

"Cool!"

At the mention of a walk, Storm twirled his tail eagerly. He skipped invisibly after Della as she and her mom set out.

A path at the side of their villa snaked down the hillside. It was very hot. Lush vines covered with pink and purple blossoms trailed over fences and the sides of buildings.

A large blue butterfly rose from the grass. Storm yapped excitedly as he launched himself at it, but then he tripped over his own paws and collapsed in a furry heap. Jumping to his feet, he shook himself before ambling off to explore a patch of wildflowers.

Della felt a bubble of laughter rising in her chest and quickly turned it into a cough. Sometimes it was hard to believe that Storm was really a magnificent young wolf!

A warm breeze blew toward them, bringing the sound of laughter and splashing from the villa that Della had glimpsed from her bedroom window.

"Anyone want a cold drink?" called a woman's voice.

"It sounds like another American family is staying there," Mrs. Walton said.

"Can we go and say hello?" Della asked eagerly, hoping the family had children.

Her mom went to knock on the door. It was opened by a woman with curly hair and a friendly smile. As Della's mom and the other woman were introducing themselves, a blond girl ran out and came toward Della and Storm. She looked about eleven years old and was wearing pink shorts over a striped halter-neck swimsuit.

Della recognized her at once. It was the girl who had been hiding in the bushes in Maria's garden! "Hi!" she called to her. "Are you staying here?"

The girl smiled and nodded. "This is our villa. Hey, I know you! You're the girl I saw yesterday. I was bored, so I sneaked into Maria's garden and hid in that bush as a joke. You should have seen your face when I was chucking those olives at you! I'm Honey, Honey Green, by the way."

"Hi, I'm Della Walton. I almost fell over when I saw your face looking out at me!" she said, grinning.

Honey laughed and tossed back
her long blond hair. "So, where are you
staying?"

"In the villa just up the hill."

"Great! So we can do stuff together,"
Honey said.

Della was delighted. Maybe Honey
could be the friend she'd been hoping
to make!

"Do you like swimming?" Honey asked.

"Yeah! I love it. But we can't use our
pool until it's been cleaned." Della made
a face as she explained about the mix-up
with their arrival date.

"Oh, what a pain!" Honey said. "You
must be really frustrated. I know! Why
don't you come and use our pool. Mom
and Dad won't mind. You can take a swim
right now . . ."

"Hold your horses, Honey. We're just about to go out, remember?" Mrs. Green smiled at her daughter and then turned back to Della. "But you're welcome anytime, Della. Why don't you come over tomorrow?"

"Thanks. I'd love to!" Della beamed,

looking forward to her first swim and to
spending time with Honey.

Della and her mom said their good-
byes and started back to their villa.

"Well, you two girls seemed to
be getting on very well," Mrs. Walton
commented. "Honey seems very . . .
lively."

"Yeah, I think she's really nice!"
Della enthused. She'd never met anyone
who was brave enough to hide in a
bush and chuck olives at people before!
But Della decided that it had actually
been quite funny, and that's definitely
what she was looking forward to this
vacation—fun!

Storm ambled alongside Della with
his tail wagging and his pink tongue
lolling out. There was a smudge of

yellow pollen on his nose. Della smiled fondly at him, imagining the good time that she, Storm, and Honey were going to have together.

Chapter
FIVE

"Can I go visit Honey?" Della asked her mom the following day. "I'm dying for a swim!"

"Maybe later, dear. We're going food shopping now."

Della was about to protest when she remembered that she needed buy Storm some food with her allowance money. "Okay, then," she said, swallowing her impatience. "I'll just get my book bag."

Storm ran upstairs with her. Della opened her bag and put it on the floor for Storm to get inside. "I think you'll be safer in here," she told him. "Do you mind?"

"It is no problem!"

Della laughed as Storm took a flying leap, jumped straight in, and curled up

next to her teddy-bear-shaped purse.

It was a short car ride to the nearest town. The big supermarket was on a side street and easy to find.

"I'll have to make sure they don't see me buying dog food," Della whispered to Storm as her mom and dad began wheeling trolleys around. "I'm going to get some . . . um, postcards and stuff," she said in a louder voice, scooting off toward the pet-care section.

Once there, she grabbed a packet of dog food and immediately headed for the checkout line.

A sudden thought struck her. "Oh, no! I only have American money," she whispered. "But I can't ask Mom or Dad to pay or they'll see what I'm buying. What am I going to do?"

"Do not worry. I will take care of it!" Storm woofed.

Della nodded. She couldn't see how Storm could solve her problem, but she trusted him so she stayed in line.

There were four people with loaded carts in front of them. Della chewed at her lip, fidgeting impatiently.

"I wish they'd hurry up. Mom and Dad are going to spot me at any moment," she whispered.

She felt a faint prickling sensation flow down her spine and tiny gold sparks glinted in Storm's fluffy ginger-and-black fur. Suddenly there was a flash of light and an invisible wave of sparkles swept Della forward to the front of the queue. "Oooh!" she exclaimed.

But no one seemed to have noticed

anything odd.

"*Hola.*" The smiling cashier scanned the dog food.

"Um . . . *hola*," Della answered nervously. She reached into her bag and opened her purse. Her eyes widened as she saw that her American money had magically transformed into euros!

She paid and slipped the bulky pack of dog food into her bag, where it instantly shrank to the size of a single bag of chips.

"Wow! That was brilliant," Della whispered to Storm as she went back into the store.

Storm showed his teeth in a doggy grin. "I am glad I could help."

They were only just in time. Della's mom and dad were in a nearby aisle, choosing a breakfast cereal. They saw her and waved.

"Pass your postcards over here, honey. We didn't get you any Spanish money yet, did we?" her dad called.

"Oh . . . I . . . um, forgot that. Silly me!" Della fibbed, walking toward them.

After the groceries had been dumped in the trunk of their car, Della, Storm, and her parents wandered around the town square. Storm looped his front paws over the sides of Della's book bag, craning his neck to check out all the sights.

Trees cast shade over outside stalls. And a delicious smell wafted from where a man in a striped apron was cooking paella in a huge cast-iron pan.

Storm sniffed, his little button nose twitching, and licked his lips hungrily.

Della got the message. "Can we try some of this, Dad?"

Mr. Walton blinked at her. "Really? Wouldn't you rather have pizza or chicken nuggets?"

"*Da-ad!* That's not all I eat," Della said, nudging him playfully. "I feel like trying something different."

They sat at a wooden bench to eat bowls of the spicy rice, fish, and vegetable mixture. Della sorted out a particularly large, juicy shrimp for Storm and put it on the bench beside him. He crunched it up with his little back teeth, his head on one side and one eye screwed shut in enjoyment.

Della's lips curved in a secret smile.

She loved having Storm for her friend.

When they got back to their villa an hour or so later, Honey was just walking up to their front drive. She had come to invite Della over for a swim. "Mom and Dad said you're invited, too," she said, smiling at Della's parents.

"Yay! Let's go!" Della said eagerly, looking at her mom and dad. She was going to get a chance to swim—at last!

"That sounds great," Mrs. Walton agreed. "Thank you, Honey. Why don't you girls go ahead? We'll put the shopping away and follow you."

Della could hardly wait. Dashing upstairs, she grabbed her bathing suit, and then she, Storm, and Honey strolled over to the Greens' villa.

A droning, buzzing sound—like someone running their nails across ridged cardboard—filled the hot air. "That's the cicadas. They're like fat grasshoppers," Honey said. "They're harmless. In some parts of the world, people *eat* them! Can you believe it?"

"Yuck!" Della screwed up her face, impressed by Honey's knowledge.

At the villa, she quickly got changed. Honey's mom and dad were relaxing on lounge chairs. They waved cheerfully as the girls came out into the garden.

"Last one in eats a cicada burger!" yelled Honey as she raced toward the pool, hotly pursued by Della.

There was a huge splash as they both jumped in.

Storm sprawled on his side with his

pink tongue hanging out as he cooled
off in the shade while Honey and Della
messed around doing handstands in the
shallow end. After that, they swam some
laps and then Della decided to float about
on her back for a while.

Honey had other ideas. She
climbed out, scrunched into a ball, and
cannonballed into the water—right by
Della. "Geronimo!"

A big wave slopped all over Della.

"You meanie!" Della said, laughing.
"Don't do that. I'm relaxing."

"Tough!" Honey's eyes flashed with mischief. She climbed out and cannonballed near Della again.

This time Della kicked away strongly and just managed to avoid being swamped. "Honey!"

Honey took no notice. She jumped in time after time, splashing almost right on top of Della. After being cannonballed for about the tenth time, Della's eyes were stinging. She coughed, spitting out water.

"*Hon-ey*! Stop it! It's not funny anymore!" she spluttered, completely fed up now.

Honey had surfaced, dripping, a big grin on her face. "I think it is!"

Della knew that her parents would have stepped in and taken charge, but Honey's mom and dad seemed to let Honey do just what she wanted to. Della gave up. Pulling herself out of the pool, she went over and spread her towel next to Storm.

The tiny puppy was dozing, his little paws flexing as he dreamed of chasing rabbits. He opened one sleepy blue eye and wagged his tail when Della threw herself onto her tummy.

"Aw! Come on back in. It was only a joke. Don't be such a wimp!" Honey jeered.

"In a little while," Della said. "Promise." She wanted Honey to think she was having fun so they'd hang out together again, but for now she needed a bit of a break. Honey wasn't like most of Della's other friends!

Chapter
SIX

When Della awoke the following morning, bars of sunlight were streaming in through the partially opened shutters.

Her mom and dad had decided to have a quiet day reading and relaxing by the pool. They suggested that Della might like to invite Honey over.

"Cool!" Della and Storm went to the Greens' villa right after breakfast.

Honey was delighted. "I've got a great idea!" she said, stopping dead as they were walking back up the hillside. "Follow me!"

"Where are we going?" Della asked, a little wary after yesterday.

"You'll see," Honey said, starting to jog in the opposite direction.

Della hung back and the still-invisible Storm paused beside her. "I thought we were going back to my place. I ought to tell Mom and Dad if we're going anywhere else. They're *really* strict about that."

Honey rolled her eyes. "Don't freak out! Jeez! We'll only be gone for a few minutes."

Della hesitated, but it was really hard to say no to Honey. She had a way of making her feel silly and fussy. "Well—okay then. If we're quick," she decided.

They set off again and soon came in sight of a familiar building. It was Maria Isola's farm.

"I'm not hiding in the garden and chucking things at people," Della said, guessing that was what Honey had in mind.

"As if! Been there, done that," Honey scoffed. "I've got a much better idea." She dashed across the field and went into the grove of orange and lemon trees.

Della followed more slowly. She didn't feel quite right about being there.

"We're going to have a climbing contest!" Honey sang out. She grabbed a low branch and rapidly climbed upward. Oranges fell out of the tree and bounced

on to the grass. "See, easy-peasy! Your
turn! Go on—climb that one," Honey
urged, pointing.

Della stood there, undecided. Maybe
she should just go back to her villa,
but then Honey would think she was a
pathetic wimp.

Storm looked up at her. "What do you
want to do?" he woofed.

"I guess I'll *have* to climb up," Della
whispered to him.

Storm's furry brow wrinkled in a
frown. "Are you good at climbing?"

"I've never tried. I don't like heights
much," Della admitted.

"Come on! What are you waiting for?"
Honey called.

Della swallowed hard. Reaching up,
she grasped a branch and felt around for a

foothold. Bracing herself against the trunk, she heaved herself upward. Climbing was harder than she'd expected, but with a lot of puffing and panting she finally managed to scramble into the tree.

"Phew!" Della clung on tight, feeling quite pleased with herself. Maybe Honey was right and this was going to turn out to be fun.

But when she looked down through the branches at Storm, he seemed a long way below her and looked even tinier than usual. His bright-blue eyes were full of concern.

Della started to feel dizzy and there was a swirling feeling in her head.

Honey crowed with laughter from the nearby tree. "Gotcha! I never thought you'd do it!" She swiftly climbed back down and jumped to the ground. "See ya!" she called, racing back across the field and disappearing.

"Hey! Wait for . . . Oh, great," Della groaned. Her heart sank as she realized that Honey had played a trick on her.

There was a movement from near the farmhouse. Someone began walking toward the trees.

Panicking, Della started to climb down, but in her hurry she lost her footing and her legs dangled in midair. She tried to hang on to a branch, but her fingers weren't strong enough and started slipping.

"Eek!" Della gulped as her tummy lurched. She was going to fall!

Suddenly Della felt a warm tingling feeling down her spine, stronger than last time, as bright golden sparks ignited in Storm's fluffy ginger-and-black fur and tiny lightning bolts fizzed from his ears and tail.

Della plunged downward surrounded by a silent whirlwind of golden sparks,

which swirled around her like tiny worker bees. She tensed, ready for a jolt of pain, but instead of the bruising landing that she expected, Della fell on to a deep pile of squishy green velvet cushions.

Plop! Plop! Plop! Oranges bounced down beside her, knocked off the branches by her fall.

A voice rang out as someone came closer. "Della? Are you all right?" Maria's face was creased with concern.

Della felt the velvet cushions disappear one by one. She sat up on the grass, unable to believe that she hadn't hurt herself.

Storm ran up, jumped into her lap and started licking her face.

"Thanks, Storm," Della whispered, moving him gently aside as she struggled to her feet. "I'm okay!" she said in a louder voice so that Maria could hear her.

"I am glad. You can help yourself
to oranges whenever you like," Maria
said gently. "But maybe you should ask
Carmella to help you pick them."

"I wasn't picking ora—" Della
stopped herself. "I was . . . We were . . .
I mean . . ." she stammered and then fell
silent. She was furious with Honey, but
she wasn't prepared to tattle on her, even
if it would get herself out of trouble. "I'm
really sorry," she finished miserably.

"I accept your apology. Let us say no
more about it," Maria said, patting her
arm. "Are you sure that you were alone
just now?"

Della nodded, mutely, her face
burning.

"Very well. I do not think I need to

tell your parents about this," Maria said
kindly. "Off you go, Della."

Storm trotted alongside her as she
walked quickly across the field without
turning back. She felt awful about lying
to Maria, but she didn't think she had
much choice.

Honey was waiting for her a bit
farther on. "You took your time. What
happened?"

"Maria thought I was stealing oranges.
She said I could have as many as I like. I
only had to ask."

"That's hilarious!" Honey clapped
her hands to her mouth and burst out
laughing.

Della didn't think it was funny and
was still too annoyed about Honey's mean
trick to talk to her just then. She marched

up the hillside toward her villa with Storm, leaving Honey to follow her.

"It was only a joke! You didn't get in too much trouble, did you?" Honey called after her. "Look, I'm sorry, Della. Let's still be friends?"

Della sighed and stopped, waiting for Honey to catch up. She guessed that, even with Storm keeping her company, the vacation would definitely be more interesting with Honey around.

Honey looked at Della solemnly. "I'm glad you got down the tree safely. Otherwise you'd be orange juice!"

The two girls burst into giggles and carried on back up the hill together.

Chapter
SEVEN

The following day the two families had planned a shared trip to the seaside. Della was really looking forward to it. She had decided to forget about yesterday and hoped Honey wasn't in too much of a joke-playing mood.

She began putting some last-minute things into her shoulder bag. "Bathing suit, towel, dog food for Storm," she said, mentally ticking things off. "Oh, where are my other flip-flops?"

"I will find them," Storm woofed helpfully, diving into the bottom of her wardrobe and emerging with a flip-flop dangling from his mouth.

"Thanks, Storm." Della smiled at him as she took the now slightly damp shoe and then reached in for the other one. Her fingers closed on something big and leggy.

"Aaargh!" Della shrieked, shooting backward and sitting down hard on her behind.

Yipe! Taken by surprise, Storm almost jumped out of his fur.

He leaped into the wardrobe again and came out carrying the most enormous plastic spider Della had ever seen. Shaking his head and growling, he tossed it across the room.

"It's okay. It's not real," Della spluttered, laughing now that her heartbeat had returned to normal. "Honey must have sneaked up here yesterday and put it there. It *was* pretty funny. I don't mind jokes like that. I bet they heard me screaming in America!" She shook her head slowly as she finished packing her bag.

"The Greens are here. Are you ready, Della?" Mr. Walton called up the stairs.

"Coming!" Della and Storm ran down, went outside and piled into the back of the Greens' car. Honey was already in the back. Della plonked down next to her.

"Thanks for the *pet* spider! It was a bit *small*. Couldn't you find a bigger, blacker, hairier one?" she joked.

"What spider?" Honey tried to look innocent, but she couldn't help grinning. "I couldn't resist it. Glad you liked it. I've brought my new kite with me," she said, changing the subject. "I hope it's windy enough to fly it. We can take turns with it."

"Sounds great. Thanks, Honey," she said, touched by the other girl's generosity. This was the Honey she really liked and wanted to be friends with.

Della sat stroking Storm, who was on the seat beside her, nearest the car door. After a while he stood up on his little back legs to look out of the window, his ears flapping in the breeze.

They reached the coast twenty minutes later. Mrs. Green parked the car and they all walked the few yards to a wide beach with pale, silvery sand. Creamy-topped waves were gently rolling in and breaking on the shore.

It was very hot, but there was a strong breeze blowing.

"Perfect for kite-flying later," Honey announced.

Storm's nose twitched as he smelled the salty air. His little paws kicked up spurts of sand as he scampered invisibly after Della.

The moms set up a striped beach umbrella, and the dads went off to buy everyone ice cream. While they were waiting for them to return, Honey and Della made a sand castle.

The castle of heaped sand was soon

patted into shape, but it was still a bit
lumpy. Honey thought it was in need of
a tower or two, but they didn't have any
buckets with them to make some.

"At least we can make a moat," Della
said. Storm came and stood very close to
her hands, so he could enjoy digging, too,
without Honey noticing. His little paws
pedaled like fury and he yapped with
enjoyment as sand flew everywhere.

"Wow! You work fast!" Honey said,
impressed, as Della appeared to have dug a
moat in record time.

"Yeah, I do, don't I?" Della replied,
grinning.

The dads arrived with ice cream. Della
and Honey sat on the sand to eat theirs.
Della sneaked a fingerful of ice cream to
Storm when no one was looking.

Honey finished hers first. She
looked sideways at Della and a familiar
mischievous expression crossed her face.
Reaching out, Honey snatched her half-
finished ice cream.

"Hey!" Della cried.

She watched in disbelief as Honey
leaped to her feet and dumped the half-
eaten cone upside down on top of their
sandcastle. "Perfect. One pointed tower!"

"Why didn't you use your own cone? I was enjoying that!" Della grumbled.

"Ha-ha! I'll buy you another one," Honey laughed.

"Don't bother!" Della stomped down to the shore, where she paddled about by herself in the cool water. "Honey just can't help herself! She makes me so mad!"

Storm was nodding sympathetically when he was almost drenched by an incoming wave. Barking furiously at the sea, he dodged backward to keep from getting his paws wet.

Della felt her mood lifting as she laughed at his antics. Storm always seemed to find a way to cheer her up, even when he didn't mean to!

"Della! Do you want a turn with my kite?" Honey yelled, waving.

Della looked up the beach. She shrugged. "Might as well. No sense in holding a grudge. Come on, Storm," she called softly.

When Della reached her, Honey held out the kite and a long length of string, but she kept hold of the reel with the rest of the string wrapped around it. The kite was shaped like a blue-and-orange butterfly and had two long, flowing tails.

Della reached out and took hold of the butterfly wings.

"I will hold it for you!" Storm woofed helpfully. He grabbed one of the kite's long tails in his teeth.

"No, don't! It could be dangerous . . . ," Della cautioned, realizing that Storm probably hadn't seen a kite before and might not know how it worked.

It was too late. "Okay, go!" Honey ordered, and pulled down hard on the kite strings just as it billowed in a gust of wind, deliberately jerking it out of Della's hands. The orange-and-blue butterfly flapped as it began to rise, with Storm still dangling from its long tail.

Chapter
EIGHT

Storm gave a muffled whine of alarm as he hung from the kite's tail.

"Hey! Where did that puppy come from?" Honey shouted.

Della realized that Storm was so scared that he must have forgotten to keep himself invisible. She didn't think twice.

One step. Two steps. Three steps. She leaped high into the air. *Yes!* Della just

managed to grab hold of Storm around
his middle. "I've got you!"

The tiny puppy let go of the kite,
which zoomed straight up into the air
until it was flying high above them.

Della landed awkwardly and twisted
her ankle. "Oh!" she gasped as a sharp pain
took her breath away. She lay on her side
on the sand, holding the shocked puppy.

Across the beach, Honey was rooted in
place with her mouth hanging open.

"Thank you for saving me, Della,"
Storm woofed.

"I'm just glad you're all right. I couldn't bear anything to happen to you." She winced. Her entire leg seemed to be aching, and she couldn't move.

Storm's midnight blue eyes widened. "You are hurt. I will make you better."

Della felt a familiar tingling down her spine as Storm hid behind her and, once again, became invisible. He then opened his mouth and huffed out a cloud of tiny gold sparks as fine as gold dust. The glittering mist swirled around Della's leg. Her ankle felt very hot for a second, and then it turned ice cold. Finally, the pain completely drained away as if it was being carried out to sea by the tide.

"Thanks, Storm. I'm fine now," Della said. She rolled over and got to her feet, just as Honey thrust the kite-reel at a nearby boy and ran up to her.

"Oh, my gosh! What happened? Where's that puppy gone? Have you hurt yourself?" she asked, her face pale.

Della took a deep breath. She could just about cope with Honey's annoying tricks and teasing ways, but it was a different matter when they put Storm in danger.

"I don't know where the puppy went. It ran away. But I've really had it with you! What kind of cruel person gets their laughs from making someone else feel angry and upset?" she fumed. "I'm not hurt, but I could have been. You're so silly! You never think about anyone but yourself!"

"I . . .I . . ." Honey opened and closed her mouth. Two bright spots of

color glowed on her cheeks. She looked
shocked and had obviously never thought
about it like that.

Della didn't wait for a reply. She
walked past Honey, stormed up the beach,
and threw herself down on the sand. She
needed time to calm down.

Storm followed her. He laid his chin on her knee and looked at her with big solemn eyes. "I do not think that Honey is a bad person."

"Me, neither. I do like her. If only she'd stop being such a pest. I really don't think Honey understands how awful it feels to have pranks played on you all the time." She sadly stroked Storm's fluffy, sun-warmed fur. "Well, I've done it now. Honey will probably never speak to me again. Thank goodness I've got you. You're a real friend. I hope you'll live with me forever."

A serious expression crossed Storm's pointed little face. "That is not possible. I must return to my home world one day, to fight Shadow and force him to leave our lands. I will become the leader of the

Moon-claw pack. Do you understand that, Della?"

Della nodded. She felt a pang of regret. She didn't think she'd ever be ready to lose her amazing puppy friend. "But that won't be for a long time, will it?" she asked.

"I do not know, but I will stay as long as I can," Storm woofed softly.

"That's okay then." Della forced all thoughts of his leaving out of her mind. She decided that she was going to enjoy every single moment she could with Storm. She jumped up and ran across the sand. "Come on, let's go exploring for shells!"

Della didn't see Honey the following day. She was starting to feel a little bad about yelling at her, even though Honey had unknowingly put Storm in danger. But it was too late for Della to take back what she'd said.

Della decided to spend the day lazing by the pool with Storm instead. Her mom came up to where she was lying on a lounge chair, reading under an umbrella.

"Aren't you going to meet up with Honey today?" she asked.

Della shook her head.

Mrs. Walton looked thoughtful. "Did you two have a fight or something?"

"Not exactly," Della said evasively. "Maybe I'll see her later." *Or she might come talk to me*, she found herself thinking hopefully.

The day after, there was still no sign of Honey, so that afternoon Della and Storm visited a medieval hill-town with her mom and dad.

There was a fiesta, celebrating the birthday of the town's patron saint. The tall buildings of sand-colored stone were strewn with flags and ribbons, and a band led a colorful parade.

A large splashing stone fountain helped cool the hot air. Della and Storm nibbled at some *churros*, long thin doughnuts, as they watched people in costumes holding up a picture of a woman in long robes, decorated with flowers.

"I bet Honey would have loved this," Della said wistfully.

Storm nodded.

It was late when they got back, and Della went straight up to bed. "Sweet dreams," she said, cuddling Storm in the darkness. A loud growling and snapping sound from outside woke her an hour later. Della shot upright and switched on her bedside lamp.

She reached out to see if Storm was awake, but he wasn't on the bed. "Storm?" she whispered.

There was no answer. *Where could he be?*

C h a p t e r
NINE

Della heard a tiny whine of terror. It was coming from under the bed.

She jumped out and bent down to look beneath it. Storm was curled into a tiny ball, pressed up against the wall. She saw that the little puppy was trembling.

"What's wrong? Are you sick?" she asked worriedly.

"I sense that Shadow knows where I

am. I heard those dogs outside and I think he has sent them after me," he whimpered.

Della felt a stir of alarm, but the barking and growling was already beginning to fade, and soon everything was silent, except for the odd buzz of the cicadas. She went over to the window and opened the shutters a crack so that she could peer out.

"There aren't any there now. Maybe it was just the farm dogs," she told him. "How will I know they're Shadow's dogs, if he does send any?"

Storm lifted his head. "They will be ordinary dogs, with fierce pale eyes and extra-long, sharp teeth. Shadow's magic will make any dog I meet into my enemy now."

"Then I'll have to make extra sure to

keep you well hidden," Della said. She reached right under the bed with one hand and gently stroked Storm with her fingertips.

The terrified puppy slowly uncurled. He crawled toward her with his ears flattened and little tummy pressed to the ground.

Della gently picked him up and got back into bed with him. She could feel his heart beating rapidly against her fingers.

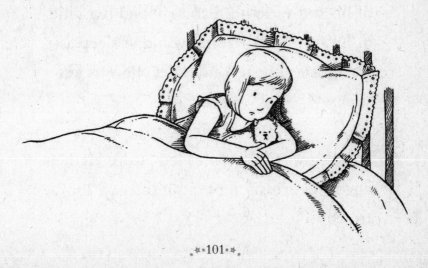

"You're safe now," she crooned. "I
hope that horrible Shadow will keep on
going and never be seen again!"

Storm twisted around to look up at
her, his little pointed face serious. "He
will never stop looking for me. If he
comes back I may have to leave suddenly,
without saying good-bye."

Della nodded sadly as she was
reminded again that she couldn't keep
Storm with her forever. She kissed the top
of his soft little head and rubbed her chin
in his fur, sure that she wouldn't sleep a
wink now. But seconds later she was fast
asleep.

"*Hola!*" Carmella called at the kitchen
door, her arms full of clean towels. "How
are you?"

Della was helping herself to orange
juice from the fridge. She looked up
and smiled at the Spanish girl. "Hi! I'm
fine, thanks."

Carmella smiled back. She came inside
and had a word with Della's mom, who
was in the front room writing postcards.

After a few minutes, Carmella
reappeared with the laundry. She paused
on her way out to speak to Della. "See
you tonight for the barbecue at the farm!
You are all invited."

"Great. See you there," Della said.
She turned to Storm when Carmella had
gone. "Sounds like fun!" she whispered
and she had a thought. "I wonder if
Honey will be there."

Storm looked up at her with his
sparkling blue eyes. "I hope so. That would

be fun." There had been no more signs of any fierce dogs, and Storm seemed back to his usual self.

Della wondered what would happen if she and Honey met up again. It was three days since the beach trip. Would Honey be glad to see her? Or would she just ignore her?

"Maybe I should go over to the villa and talk to her. Or I could write a note and slip it under the door," Della said to Storm. "I can't decide what to do. What do you think?"

Storm put his head on one side. "What do you want to do?" he woofed.

Della was silent for a moment. "I want to be friends with her again," she said finally. It was true, she realized. She missed Honey. "I know—I'll buy her a present! I can give it to her at the barbecue."

Storm nodded. "I think Honey would like that."

Della went to find her mom to ask if they could drive into town. Mrs. Walton agreed readily. "I want to get some stamps and mail these cards anyway."

Della and Storm went into a shop

with her. There was a display of stuffed animals, and Della immediately pounced on a gorgeous, realistic-looking Labrador puppy toy. It had plushy cream fur and melting brown eyes.

"Any girl would love this," she said, reaching for her teddy-bear-shaped purse.

Storm nodded agreement.

"What a cute toy. I didn't know that you were so into puppies," her mom commented as they returned to the car.

"Oh, I am—hugely!" Della said, grinning. If only her mom knew! "But it's not for me. It's for Honey."

"Ah. I see," her mom said, sounding as if she understood completely.

Della could hardly wait for the barbecue. As soon as it was dark, they all strolled down the hillside to Maria's farm.

Guitar music floated toward them. Strings of colored lights glowed from the trees, and a delicious smell rose from the barbecue, where meat was sizzling. Maria, her husband, and Carmella welcomed them. Farm workers stood around chatting and smiling in a friendly manner.

Della looked around for Honey, but the Green family hadn't arrived yet. "I hope Honey's coming," Della whispered to Storm, looking at the toy Labrador.

There was no reply.

With a whine of terror, Storm raced toward the grove of orange and lemon trees.

Della whipped around and saw two small dogs running into the courtyard. They raised their heads and she saw their abnormally long teeth and fierce pale eyes.

Her heart skipped a beat. They were here for Storm! Her friend was in terrible danger. Della dashed toward the trees. Just as she reached them, there was a bright golden flash. She blinked as her sight cleared. Storm stood there as his real wolf self. His dazzling silver-gray fur gleamed with bright sparks, and his midnight blue eyes glowed like jewels. A she-wolf with a gentle face and kind eyes stood next to him.

And then Della knew that Storm was leaving for good.

A sob rose in her throat, but she forced herself to be brave for her friend's sake. "Your enemies are close. Save yourself, Storm!"

Storm raised a large silver paw in farewell. "You have been a good friend.

Thank you for helping me, Della," he said in a deep, velvety growl.

There was an ache in Della's chest, and her eyes stung with tears. She was going to miss Storm terribly. "Good-bye. Take care. I'll never forget you," she whispered hoarsely.

There was a final bright flash, and a silent explosion of sparks sprinkled harmlessly around her like glittering sand.

Storm and his mother faded and then disappeared. The mean dogs ran through the trees. Della saw their teeth and eyes instantly return to normal before they turned and slunk away.

Della blinked away tears as she went slowly back toward the farmhouse. At least she'd had a chance to say good-bye to Storm. She knew she'd never forget the wonderful adventure she'd shared with the magic puppy.

"I know you'll be a wonderful leader some day. The Moon-claw pack is lucky to have you," she said breathlessly.

A figure ran toward her. "There you are! This is for you," Honey said. She held out a toy puppy with fluffy ginger-and-black fur. "It reminded me of that puppy on the beach."

"I absolutely love it!" Della said, gathering the toy into her arms. "I bought something for you too." She gave Honey the Labrador puppy.

"Wow! Thanks. It's adorable!" Honey gave a shaky smile. "So—does this mean we're friends again? I'm so sorry, Della."

"Definitely friends again. But no more silly pranks. Okay?" She remembered the

plastic spider in her wardrobe. "This isn't a trick puppy, is it?"

"Not exactly!" Honey showed Della the secret pocket, like a tiny furry pouch, which had a small card inside. On it was printed I AM YOUR SPECIAL FRIEND. MY NAME IS . . . There was a gap to write the name of your choice.

"No contest. I know exactly what I'm going to call my puppy!" Della said, her heart lifting, as she linked arms with Honey.

About the
AUTHOR

Sue Bentley's books for children often include animals, fairies, and wildlife. She lives in Northampton, England, and enjoys reading, going to the movies, relaxing by her garden pond, and watching the birds feeding their babies on the lawn. At school she was always getting yelled at for daydreaming or staring out of the window—but she now realizes that she was storing up ideas for when she became a writer. She has met and owned many cats and dogs, and each one has brought a special kind of magic to her life.

Don't miss these Magic Puppy books!

Don't miss these Magic Kitten books!

#1 A Summer Spell

#2 Classroom Chaos

#3 Star Dreams

#4 Double Trouble

#5 Moonlight Mischief

#6 A Circus Wish

#7 Sparkling Steps

#8 A Glittering Gallop

#9 Seaside Mystery

#10 Firelight Friends

#11 A Shimmering Splash

A Christmas Surprise

Purrfect Sticker
and Activity Book

Starry Sticker
and Activity Book

Don't miss these Magic Ponies books!

Don't miss these Magic Bunny books!

#1 Chocolate Wishes

#2 Vacation Dreams

#3 A Splash of Magic

#4 Classroom Capers

#5 Dancing Days